# Yeshua:

# *Stories of Jesus the Christ*

# YESHUA:

# Stories of Jesus the Christ

*by Maudeen Grace Jordan*

# DEDICATION

I dedicate this book
to my eternal spiritual friends,
my Gurus and Guides,
the Lord Jesus Christ
first known as Yeshua
and
Paramahansa Yogananda
who deeply loved and revered him.
Their wisdom and love infused me
with the desire to know more
of the personal Jesus or Yeshua,
as a friend to all.

I also dedicate this book to my mother
Florence Harriet Nicholson
who taught me how to pray
to a loving Father God
and set a strong example of determination,
focus and following your heart's dream.

# INTRODUCTION

Yeshua is Hebrew for Jesus. It is the name that the angels gave to Mary and Joseph to call their son; it means Savior. "Yeshua is called Iesous in Greece, Jesus (hey-soos) in Spanish-speaking countries, Issa in Tibet, Isa in India and Isha is a name used by the Wise Men, which means Lord. Jesus the Christ spoke in the Aramaic dialect and his family most likely would have pronounced his name Eshu."[1]

Likewise, Yeshua's mother was Miriam in the original Hebrew and Miriam or Maryam in the Aramaic language. English-speakers call her Mary and Spanish-speakers call her Maria.

This little book contains stories from a Jewish woman's point of view that could have happened during the time of Yeshua. The spiritual principles in these stories are based on the teachings of Paramahansa Yogananda founder of Self-Realization Fellowship. Primarily I have used as my guides his _Autobiography of a Yogi_ and _The Second Coming of Christ -The Resurrection of the Christ Within You_.

In _Study Notes_ and _Further Study Notes in Relationship to Footnotes_, I have included many references to these two books in hopes that you will be encouraged to study these principles for yourself and enjoy the beautiful illustrations of Yeshua in _The Second Coming of Christ_ by Heinrich Hofmann, Carl Bloch, Bartolome Murillo and VV Sapar.

The influences on my spiritual life have been the teachings of Paramahansa Yogananda and Self-Realization Fellowship, the teachings of Unity Church founded by Charles and Myrtle Fillmore and two devotional books: _The Stories of Jesus_ by Aylesa Forsee, now out of print and in the public domain, and _He and I_ by Gabrielle Bossis. These stories are based on my intuition. I pray that they are Divinely-guided and inspired and that you enjoy them.

# WHAT READERS SAY ABOUT YESHUA

Grace . . . YOU are a very good writer! :-) Thanks so much for sharing Yeshua with me! What a delight! I looked forward to every opportunity to read it! I really love how it brought it so alive, and so current with what we know now. Instead of "way back then", it's right now, just like...well, right now! - Dambara B, Washington

"Thank you for *Yeshua*. It's really lovely—I have enjoyed every bit of it. You've done a beautiful job of describing the luminous nature of the guru and the joy and receptivity of the true disciple." - Latika P, California

"Oh my, how beautiful your words. I have just started reading and already I sense the peace, joy and all fulfilling love of Christ Jesus. Thank you, thank you, thank you for sending this to us. Your written words are infused with divinity to touch our hearts where they need to be touched at this point in our lives." - Cecile M, Indiana

"I finally was able to read your book and am quite touched by the sweet devotion with which you write. And so nice to receive as a Christmas gift! Your writing style is very warm and caring." - Lisa B, Oregon

"Maudeen, *Yeshua: Stories of Jesus* renews my sense of

joy and happiness. Your writing expresses such gentle loving kindness. It's a read and re-read study in Jesus mission on Earth." - Glenda G, Oregon

"You have created a thought-provoking work. I am so happy to see your thoughts on paper, my friend. They are beautiful . . . Yeshua became vibrant and alive."
- Lynn W, Oregon

# *ACKNOWLEDGMENTS*

I thank my husband of 35 years who proofread
my drafts and encouraged me.  What better gift to me
than to give his encouragement and empathy!

I thank my dear friend Linda Moyer
who always gave her loving and spiritual support
no matter how busy she was and
who first gave us a wedding gift of the book
*He and I* by Gabrielle Bossis.

I give special thanks to my dear friends, Lynn Walker,
who gave freely of her support, wisdom,
encouragement and clarity of thought
and
I thank Claudia Mosias who shared her editing skills
and her software program when mine was not working.

*The greatest Goal in life is to*
*experience Christ-consciousness*
*or the bliss of the Soul*
*through the daily practice of*
*God-focused meditation.*

Paramahansa Yogananda

# YESHUA: TABLE OF CONTENTS

# Chapter 1:

## Your Master Comes Today!

We had heard the most amazing stories of a man called Yeshua who healed the sick, the blind, the lame. We heard that he had turned water into wine at a wedding ceremony. We heard that he spoke words of wisdom that uplifted and inspired, unlike the rabbis' usual dry words. Some people even said that he could be our long-awaited Messiah. They called him *Yeshua HaMashiach meaning* Yeshua the Messiah or Yeshua the Savior. Could it be possible? He was just the son of a carpenter from the Nazareth. Still, we all prayed it could be he and we also hoped that he would travel near our little village; we wanted to see and hear him for ourselves.

I loved my parents and our neighbors and the One God but since the violent death of my new husband at the hand of the Romans, all purpose seemed to have left me. I lived too much in thoughts of how he had died. I longed for something more, much more, but I didn't know what would satisfy me.

As I awoke that glorious day, I had such a feeling of

divine anticipation that I could not explain. I rose to my duties as usual and suddenly heard a cry ~ *"Yeshua is here! The Messiah has come!"* As I heard his name, I dropped my bowl and its contents. It clanged loudly as it fell to the floor but I cared not at all. I felt a surge of joy and started running. As others joined me, I was jostled by the excited, hopeful crowd and those of us who could, ran full speed to see him … there, standing on a hill …

I began to feel such a deep peace that my steps began to slow… I was enthralled by his glorious, smiling face. I wanted to run to him but I only felt to sit right where I was and experience this delicious peace, like a balm.

He was speaking! Such a voice! It was such a healing voice that it seemed all Nature was stilled in that great calmness. As I sat, my eyes and gaze moved upward to what he was describing as the light of God in the body. How long I sat in that great stillness I don't know but I felt completely and fully satisfied.

Yeshua spoke of healing, that God could heal our bodies but he knew that what we really wanted was this great, living, joyous peace and that it be lasting and ever-new and living, like now. He was so right! I wasn't worried about my bodily aches or pains. I was no longer grieving. I felt no desire for anything as I sat in that glorious rightness. He said that this is the contact of the Father within, that we should sit like this every morning and every evening before bed and absorb more of *THIS!* This glowing, satisfying stillness.

He approached me, calmly walking through the crowd, touching some. I felt that I had known him before! Part of me wanted to rise and embrace him as my long-lost best friend or to touch his holy feet but as he approached, I felt even more deeply this glorious solidity, vibrant with peace and joy. He touched me on the head like a caress but also like the thunderous roar of the ocean. My awareness expanded. I felt as if I was above the crowd and one with it too. My awareness grew to include the surrounding countryside and villages. I could see within my consciousness some Roman soldiers approaching us on horseback. They had been sent to settle the "disturbance" of an entire village leaving its duties in the dust.

When they did eventually reach us, they were so surprised to find us all sitting quietly. There was no disturbance here at all and their fear and worry left them. Some slid from their saddles to stand nearby or join us on the grass, sitting among us. It seemed perfectly natural to me, a Jew, that they should do so, in the presence of this man Yeshua! My awareness returned to an appreciation of his glorious, glowing face and strong, confident stride but oh, the truth that came from him was truly the most glorious and amazing part about him!

He taught us that we are all equals in the Father's eyes and that our only true duty in this life was to keep remembering that oneness with the Father as His very own child. He explained that there was no difference between us at all in Spirit.

"Spirit," he said, "is the joy you feel right now." We felt his words in our whole being as if his words too were Spirit.

Hours passed. I only knew it because the sky began to change colors. He instructed us to go home and commune with the Father again before lying on our mats that we should come to see him again tomorrow, after our duties were done. I knew we would all most certainly return to see Yeshua. We already revered him and the tremendous gifts he had given us. He said that he wanted us to be personal friends of his! I found such relief and joy in the new Divine direction I had been given, of daily meditating and living the Truth that we are all children of the One Loving Father God.

## Chapter 2:

## *"You are welcome here."*

So easily I jumped up out of my bed to complete my duties, in such joyous expectation of seeing Yeshua again! As I quickly walked through the quiet, vibrant morning, sparkling with dew, the sun had just begun to peek over the horizon. The sound of my sandals in the crunchy gravel slowed, as I approached the spot in the orchard. 'Oh, he is here!', my heart leaped. He was sitting with a small group of people. I was enraptured by his face so full of love and light. I decided to sit at this respectful distance but no, he called my name! How could he possibly know my name? I rose and approached him. I suddenly realized that I had not meditated on the Father as he had asked. I felt ashamed.

He answered my silent thought with the questions, "But, do you love me? Do you love God and the spiritual truth that I bring?"

I answered, "Yes, sir, I do."

"Good," he answered, "but there is no need to call me sir. We are all children of the One Father, equal in His

5

sight. You are just as worthy and just as wonderful as I am or any of these dear ones here. Meditation is a science and it takes a little discipline and practice. Practice regularly and you will see improvements that you'll very much like. Sit with us now. You are welcome here!"

The unspoken directive was to go within but I stole a glance at his glorious face and the devoted faces of those around him. I thought to myself, 'He is still here. He is not going to leave! He is not making me leave. I am accepted here.' I felt loved, really loved and safe. I closed my eyes again and lifted them to feel the glowing power of the Father within.

Time passed and we became aware of excited and hopeful voices coming near. They were carrying someone. This person that they carried was full of hope. I could see it in her eyes. Her friends laid her right before Yeshua.

"Daughter," he asked, "do you believe that God can heal you through me?"

"Yes," she answered him, "with all my heart and soul, I do."

"So, you want to walk again?"

"Yes, Raboni, but heal also my heart of jealousy and envy and anger toward the one who injured me. I want to love all the time, like you do!"

"Oh, you ask for such an important healing, the only lasting kind!"

He took her hands and she easily rose and walked and then danced for joy and sang. Her delighted friends were clapping and praising God. I was astounded and simply mute but so glad for her. My old beliefs were melting way.

'All things are possible in God,' I mused. What is this new world I am living in? Who is this wonderful God-tuned man of Truth?' No matter. I never wanted to leave.

My name? Yes, he had called me. I approached Yeshua, not with fear but with reverence.

"Stay with us." he said. "You should tell your family why you are leaving and let them know that you'll share what you learn when you return in a year... and," he advised, "travel lightly."

## Chapter 3:

## *A Heavenly Home at His Feet*

"Travel lightly," he had said.  So, I grabbed a change of clothes and extra sandals and a shawl. I was also attracted to a little ball. So, I took it too. My parents had given it to me in their hope of one day having a grandchild, but I had not been blessed with a child or a long-lived husband. My aunt had easily agreed to watch over my parents for me who were now aging and slowing down but still healthy.

It felt strange to be leaving my village. I had only visited two other villages, but I loved our own for its simple devotion to the One God and its few beautiful trees that surrounded our well. We were surprised one day when the Romans galloped into the village. What could they possibly want from us? It was food. So, they took some of our sheep and goats, our best grains and seeds and figs and left the courtyard in a flurry of dust and flying chickens.

What would it be like to follow Yeshua? They had told me that Yeshua was a world traveler and had even gone east to India and the Himalayan Mountains. Well, no matter to me! If he stayed in one spot, I would gladly stay. If he traveled the world, I would gladly follow and serve him in any way I could.

I kissed my dear, dear parents good-bye. They were happy for me, bless them! Would I see them again? My love for them was very, does not often come in form. He great but my love for Yeshua and his teachings drew me like a strong need, with a joy that I had never known before!

On my way out of the village, I grabbed a flask of our fresh well water. And then, I quickly found myself in Heaven. Yeshua was playing with a large group of children. I then knew why I had brought the ball and threw it out into the center of them. There were instant squeals of laughter. I stood in amazed delight, watching Yeshua dart around, jumping and laughing just like one of the children, only taller and stronger. He had captured their hearts completely and after a while, he sat on a large rock and they crawled all over him and played with his long dark hair. He began to tell them stories, stories of courage and calmness in the face of danger and love and compassion for birds and animals and people. God had indeed sent us an anointed one. That fact I knew for certain to the center of my bones! The ball rolled over near me and I placed it in my satchel again.

At this time, Yeshua suggested that we all go to the

river to bathe, clothes and all, and then pray and meditate before dinner. I was deeply content and beyond happy to be part of this inner circle of friends.

After our meditation, he spoke to us about becoming like little children[2] and asked us what we liked about them. Children are pure and guileless, humble and full of love and joy and they have boundless trust. They are often quite free of likes and dislikes and possessiveness. Yeshua encouraged us to be as much like them as we possibly could be. He also asked that we follow him lamblike and ask questions if we really needed to ask. He promised to guide us to awareness of the Father within us. Only then could we fully receive all our inheritance from Spirit, as God's divine heirs. He called this inheritance Christ-consciousness.

My first night of sleep on the bare ground of our camp was deeply peaceful and comfortable, under the great, endless starry sky, with just my shawl and a blanket to cover me.

## Chapter 4:

## The Dawn

Early in the morning, I awoke to quiet and slowly brightening skies. Yet, there was another light as well! As I turned my gaze in the direction of the Master Yeshua, I beheld his radiantly glowing face. He sat on a large rock in deep communion with God.[3]

His whole being radiated with a light that was bright but more gentle and healing than any sunlight could ever be. It appeared to come from within him and shone out in a radiance that enveloped all of us and all Nature all around us!

I was dumbstruck with awe and reverence for him. All I could do was stare at him. Such beauty and power and divinity have never been seen in a human face before, I thought.

I have kept this chapter short to emphasize how there are no words to express how important, how earth-changing, how soul-awakening and healing this experience, this Truth was to me.

## Chapter 5:

## The Great, Bright Love of Yeshua

Waking early the next day, we sat with him for a long time in meditation. It was like a great, vibrant stillness, which was so satisfying, like a long overdue, deep sleep but so much more alive and joyous. It seemed to me that even the morning birds hushed their singing. Or was it that the world had faded in importance to me? I certainly cared not for the outside world at all.

Hours later, we began to stir with the sounds of many approaching feet and the growling of our stomachs. Yeshua responded to our thoughts and said,
"Man shall not live by bread alone but by every word that proceeds out of the mouth of God." - Matthew 4:4

Such a strange saying but I understood it completely.

He went on to say that God's love and wisdom and joy is like the sun, giving warmth and life, that His light continually shines both around us everywhere and within us, giving us food for our souls, love, joy and a reason to live. Even so, He directed one of his disciples to pass out bread and figs to all.

People began to arrive and sit in clusters around the Master. Some came with entire families. They had apparently left their homes and work to hear the Master and his new living words.

Yeshua, like God Himself, was like a great sun of unconditional love. All were drawn to him irresistibly. His love was so great that all of us longed to get as close as possible to him. To be near him was to feel totally accepted and cherished as if we were part of that same sun and even like him! In fact, he said, "You are the light of the world. A city set on a hill cannot be hidden. Neither do men light a candle and put it under a basket, but on a candlestick. It gives light to all who are in the house. Let your light so shine before men that they see your good works and glorify your Father who is in heaven."
— Matthew 5:14-16

And another truth too, he told us, "The light of the body is the eye. Therefore, if thine eye be single,[4]
thy whole body shall be full of light."    — Matthew 6:22

One meaning is that in our daily life, if we follow what is good and right, our whole body will be healthier and happier and our relations with others will improve. On the inside, he said, as we focus on the great inner sun of God or the great star within the forehead, that light feeds us with Spirit and we grow inwardly like a giant tree, reaching up to more and more light and love.

## Chapter 6:

## *Disciples of the Master*

As the days passed with so much joy and inner growth, I began to notice the ebb and flow of the inner circle. Yeshua treated us all equally: male and female, young and old, wealthy or poor, educated or illiterate, rabbi or commoner, Jew, Gentile, Sadducee or Pharisee, Zealot or Roman soldier. All were the same beautiful souls to him!

He told us that he had known us all before in past lives and that he felt a special responsibility toward us to help us reach our perfection in God. The more we followed him exactly in every detail, the more quickly we would reach our Heavenly Goal of Oneness with God.

However, when he said to some, "Follow me." it held a special significance. To those of us who followed and served him and his guests on a daily basis, he gave special in-depth explanations of his teachings and expected us to put those truths into practice immediately. And, to those to whom it was understood that they would one day carry his message, he gave even deeper instruction and expected them to have near perfect discipline, commitment and focus. To those perhaps ten or fifteen, he eventually gave even the power to heal.

He told us that we would all one day heal others, but it requires great love and faith and knowledge of certain unseen laws and a deep understanding of what the person truly needs. There were times when Yeshua did not heal people's bodies but gave them a choice to keep their malady and advance spiritually very quickly or to be healed and progress more slowly. They usually followed his advice because they felt so much better; they had found a connection in Spirit that would sustain them.

"There are certain spiritual keys," he told us. "Using our free will rightly is the first of these glorious keys."

"Be ye therefore perfect, even as your Father who is in heaven is perfect", he said. - Matthew 5:48

Since we are already his divine children, the fulfillment of perfection depends on our using our free will rightly. We must always choose the highest and kindest actions in our dealings with others and we must also be kind and compassionate with our self as we travel the spiritual road to God within.

He said that the second spiritual key is love:

He said, "You shall love the Lord thy God with all your heart, with all your soul, with all your strength and with all your mind and your neighbor as yourself." - Luke 10:27

Besides kindness and respect for others, it also means to meditate with your heart, soul, strength and mind focused on God-alone and carry that beautiful feeling and focus on God with you as you live and work in the world.

The intensity of our desire is the third key:

In other words, how deeply do we love and desire our oneness with Our Father as love, as joy, as peace? Do we yearn for the Divine Beloved to enter our thoughts, our heart, our soul, and our life?

The disciple John was the best example, in my opinion, of love and intensity. From the minute he met the master Yeshua, he had said, "I heard your words, Master, and that is what we want, to have your words written upon our hearts!" John was so enthusiastic and so full of love that he would sit next to Yeshua, meditating all the time. The Master would not request any task of him. He said that John was doing a far greater work for himself and all of us by his communion with God.

Peter was more outward in his enthusiasm for the Yeshua's spiritual truths and was a true leader to the others. Peter expressed his love in service to the Master and service to others. All the Chosen Ones had wonderful qualities and I could see why Yeshua chose them to carry the Message.

So like John, do we express our divine love and devotion to the One God, the Father Within us primarily by meditation? Or, like Peter, do we express our love primarily by serving others?

In fact, he said that we all carry God's Message of Love and Peace and Joy in our own way, by the example of how we live our lives. We have a unique way of expressing God because we are uniquely created and loved by God.

The fourth and final key is the master to all the other keys. It is meditation. [5]

Do we take *the time* to go within frequently, to pray, meditate and practice His Presence, at least upon waking and before sleep? Do we practice the meditation techniques that Yeshua taught us, by connecting to Spirit and loving Him as only we can as a unique soul? Are we taking the time to love God with all our hearts, with all our souls, with all our strength, with all our minds and to love our neighbor as ourselves?

The Chosen Ones and most of the followers of Yeshua who stayed with him for weeks at a time were men but there were also women, older women or widows like me.

Younger women were usually married with children and had caretaker duties. Yeshua encouraged mothers by telling them that their work was the most important of all, to teach faith to little receptive souls. He recommended that they teach and model for their children:

- to love God foremost in their lives and to put Him first every day by praying and meditating.

- to be brave and stand up for the truth and what is right.

- to obey the Golden Rule [5] of respecting others and doing unto others only what they themselves would want and appreciate. In these ways, they could live in the world harmoniously and have joyful lives.

The Golden Rule is: "Do unto others as you would have others do unto you." -- Luke 6:31

Of the regular followers of Yeshua, or the Christ as we began to call him, there were about twenty-five of us. We women tried to be of service in the ways in which we were familiar, cooking, cleaning and caring for others. Sometimes we would fuss and argue over what foods were good enough for him. When we served these foods to Yeshua, he would return them to us saying that they were spoiled by our thoughts of argumentativeness and worry.

He taught us to instead sing and pray to the One God as we cooked. This practice made the simplest and plainest of foods a feast of joy to the Master. He was very grateful for these foods and blessed them to good use in our bodies. With this devotional attitude, we always felt deeply satisfied with a little or a lot of food.

When someone who was not a disciple, like a rabbi or a zealot or someone in political power, such as a Roman or a Pharisee, was confrontive or threatening or rude to Yeshua, the hair on our necks rose defensively. In contrast, Yeshua was like a calm, very deep lake that no one and no circumstance could disturb. He was firm, respectful and imperturbable, no matter who or what the situation. He always gave an answer that satisfied us at a spiritual level. However, his antagonists may have been embarrassed, frustrated or angry with the same answer because he had managed to evade their efforts to discredit him. After the disturbance had past, Yeshua went right back into his joyful, loving center. In fact, I feel that he never left that consciousness. A wonderful example of his calm authority was the day he asked for a coin in answer to a question about paying homage to Caesar.

He simply replied,

"Show me a denarius.  Whose image and inscription does it have?" They answered and said "Caesar's." He said unto them, "Then render to Caesar what is Caesar's and to God what is God's." -- Luke 20:24-25

"They could not catch him in his words before the people. And they marveled at His answer and were silent." - Luke 20:26

# Chapter 7:

## The Mother of Yeshua

That wonderful lady – so deeply peaceful – so beautiful – so radiant! I was awestruck. I watched her from a distance for several days, locked in the inner communion of meditation, her face glowing with love.

One afternoon, the Master approached in my direction, arm in arm with her. They were talking and laughing like long lost friends. They walked straight up to me! Yeshua introduced me to Maryam or Mary, his mother!

Mary looked at me deeply and lovingly. I felt like she was searching for the real me. Her first words to me were "I like you!" and proceeded to ask me if she could sit with me and if I would tell her about myself.

Mary quickly found the painful spot in my heart – no child. "My dear," she said, "when Yeshua left home at a young age to visit the three Wise Men, this worked for me; perhaps it will help you too, with God's blessing. Consider all children as your own! Pour out your love, understanding, and appreciation to them, even at a distance. Just keep doing it. We are drawn to motherhood because of the opportunity to love fully but we all can love fully at all times. Whether we suckle them or not does not matter because we are all souls starving for love. Some souls are just more confused than others. Even our Roman brothers are just confused little boys on the inside. They think that power and wealth are supreme and will make them happy. But, love alone can make us happy, love for God and each other!"

Mary sat with me that afternoon as we listened to the words of wisdom and truth pouring through Yeshua from the One God. We all peacefully meditated as one Great Heart. At the end, she added, "And you will be twice blessed for loving all children because you will not expect or demand love in return."

I felt transformed and so blessed and grateful that the mother of Yeshua would talk with me. Mary returned to her home in Nazareth a few days later but I was deeply inspired by her example and her advice. From that day, I focused even more on the children who came to see Yeshua, usually with their mother or grandparents, while their father worked. I joyfully served them all as best as I could, knowing we are all equal souls. And, I put to good use the little ball!

# Chapter 8:

## True Worship

We welcomed our Shabbat or Sabbath [6] as the sun set on Friday, greeting one another with the words: "Shabbat Shalom!" or "Peace to your Sabbath!"

The women lit candles and Yeshua led us in prayers for us, for our children and for the whole world. He led Kiddush or sanctification of the wine and we shared our challah or braided bread that some thoughtful person had baked for us. As we began dipping it in salt, Yeshua reminded us, "Remember, dear friends, you are the salt of the earth." - Matthew 5:1     Your savor is especially great when you love and put Our Father God first in your lives by prayer and meditation each morning and by remembering to treat each other with love and respect on all days of the week, not just on Shabbat!"

We deeply enjoyed just being with our dear Yeshua, our Master, at his most informal, relaxed and happy, sharing stories, wonderful truths and memories of beautiful healings.  We ended our evening with joyous singing and then a deep, peaceful meditation together.

The following morning, we woke to a glorious spring Shabbat day full of birdsong. The earth glowed with health and balance.  Yeshua spoke about how every day can be a sacred Shabbat Day. It is a gift from the One God, the Father of Love. In this God-given day, we can love exactly where God has put us, enjoy our lives with those same people that He has placed around us and loving and serving the One God in them. Yeshua said service is also a great way to burn off the effects of bad actions that we have accumulated in previous lifetimes.  In India, he said, this principle is called karma.[7]

He explained karma with a parable of a seed. Good seeds or good actions produce very good fruits or good karma and bad seeds or bad actions produce very bad fruits or bad karma. Either way, our actions can help or harm our spiritual growth and will return to us like a boomerang in this life or some other lifetime as either troubles or blessings.

Yeshua said that we can love the Spirit, our Heavenly Father-Mother, with our every thought, word and movement and especially in our worship, which is to include true silence, deeper and more still than a quiet night.

This particular Shabbat, Yeshua suggested that we go to the nearby temple. We all went together. Such harmony, beauty and joy I shall never forget. We women, along with his mother Mary, came directly into the main sacred sanctuary with the men. No one thought to complain about it. We were thrilled to be there near the

Holy of Holies, the Torah. It was deeply satisfying and fulfilling to be there as a whole, undivided community and to have the words of the Torah explained by our beautiful Master who knew God personally.

We Jews had become so locked in our traditions and the usual routine, that some of the life and spontaneity had left our worship. At times, I could see in the men's faces, pride in intellectual reasoning, boredom or even worry and angst, as they tried to worship.

But in that beautiful worship service, we were one great pulsating heart of worshipers, alive with love and joy as we alternatingly silently meditated and silently listened to Yeshua speak of the inner meanings of the Torah. Then, so joyously and enthusiastically we sang to Beloved God our old favorite songs, with a new sense of their true meaning.

I cherish that memory because all Shabbats were not so harmonious. Other times that we visited temples, we women were excluded to the outer rooms as usual and arguments often arose about how dare Yeshua presume to change the Jewish traditions and The Law. "The Law is the Law," they would say, as if that answered anything at all.

We were amazed at Yeshua's endless patience with them all. Occasionally, we would see a dawning of understanding on some faces as he spoke. To me, that transformation was more of a miracle than any healing of a physical malady. To change a long-held hardened belief and attitude to a soft and yielding devotion to God was a true miraculous healing of Spirit!

He gave us a new prayer that day. We called it, "The Lord's Prayer". [8] *See also Luke 11:1-4*

Here it is as Yeshua first prayed it in the original Aramaic [9]:
"Abwoon d'bwashmaya O Birther!
Nethqadash shmakh
Teytey malkuthakh
Nehwey sebyanach aykanna d'bwashmaya aph b'arha.
Habwlan lachma d'sunqanan yaomana.
Washboqlan khaubayn (wakhtahayn) aykana daph khnan shbwoqan l'khayyabayn.
Wela tahlan l'nesyuna
Ela patzan min bisha
Metol dilakhie malkuthat wahayla wateshbukhta l'ahlam almin. Ameyn."

Here is a translation in English [9]:
"O Birther, Father-Mother of the Cosmos, you create all that moves in light.
Focus your light within us -- make it useful as the rays of a beacon show the way.
Create your reign of unity now – through our fiery hearts and willing hands.
Your one desire then acts with ours, as in all light,

so in all forms.

Grant what we need each day in bread and insight: subsistence for the call of growing life.

Loose the cords of mistakes binding us, as we release the strands we hold of others' guilt.

Don't let us enter into forgetfulness but free us from unripeness.

From you is born all-ruling will, the power and the life to do, the song that beautifies all, from age to age it renews.

Truly — power to these statements — may they be the source from which all my actions grow.

Sealed in trust and faith.  Amen."

Later that evening, we talked about how wonderful the day had been, worshiping God in the temple together, praying, singing, meditating, learning true meanings of the Torah and praying our new prayer from the Lord.

Yeshua replied that indeed places of worship, temples, synagogues, mosques, churches, all hold sacred vibrations of our prayers and spiritual efforts. He said their holiness makes it easier to go within to worship but he asked us to always remember the real temple:

"You are the temple of God and the Spirit of God dwells in you. The temple of God is holy. And you are His Temple." — 1 Corinthians 3:16-17

To illustrate, Yeshua told us a lovely story from his youth:

"The time finally arrived for my family and our neighbors to make our annual pilgrimage to Jerusalem for the Passover. As with all Jews, Passover has always been my favorite time of year and it has always thrilled me to anticipate being in the holy city, especially in the Temple. We all thought it might be the most sacred place in the world."

"That year was very special indeed because I would be allowed to read from the Torah as a full Jewish adult. Our trip from Nazareth usually took about 5 days. Around the third day of our travels, my friends and I could not contain our excitement anymore. We got permission to go ahead of the group. The agreement was to meet in the canyon."

"We ran most of the way and finally reached the beautiful canyon of Wadi Qelt with its cascade of spring flowers and gently moving water. We drank our fill and bathed in the clear, refreshing water. And then, since we liked to pray and worship together, we sat to meditate and feel the Presence of the One God."

"We spent a long time in inner stillness and suddenly, the One God of love blessed our efforts, giving us great treasures of peace and joy beyond our highest wishes. We realized then it wasn't necessary to go to the Temple in Jerusalem. We had already been filled spiritually. We had been correct to venerate the House of God, but even more sacred is the temple within where the Spirit of God abides in each of us!"

## *Chapter 9:*

## *Yeshua Appears When Needed*

Who was this amazing person? Some called him Messiah; others called him the devil. Everyone had a different opinion of his personality.

Here are some of the various descriptions:
    outgoing; reserved
    courteous; defiant
    a skilled carpenter; a worthless wanderer
    extraordinary; ordinary
    a miracle worker; a trickster
    smart; deluded and very strange
    caring, gentle and humble; verbally assaultive
    a very good Jew; a very bad Jew
    a man of high principles; a man of no principles
    a great teacher, a blasphemer

And the list of opinions probably goes on endlessly.

As a boy, Yeshua was very active. He was trained by his father Joseph to be an excellent carpenter and he did become one at a young age.  Everyone sought out Yeshua for his skill and artistry and friendly, careful attention. He also gave more than necessary by doing extra chores. He helped with planting of crops and the care of the animals and he cared for village children, playing with them and telling them stories with morals.

Then, he was often no-where-to-be-found and finally when he was found, often by the family dog in some remote spot, he was just sitting, eyes closed and upturned, meditating in silence or praying, reciting and singing the Psalms.

As a man, he walked from village to village, teaching and healing. He had a strong and beautiful voice and people were able to hear him teach, no matter what distance they were from him. As far as I could determine, Yeshua rarely slept but preferred instead to meditate and be within, with his Heavenly Father God.

There was also a Yeshua beyond-man ~ Yeshua the Christ who expressed Christ-consciousness. [10]

Since I saw Yeshua as my Master or guru, for me he transcended the usual mundane descriptions. His thoughts and teachings were sublime. He could teach those with varying understanding using parables and stories, knowing that stories would help us remember the truth behind them. For those of us who sought deeper understanding, he taught us how to meditate on God within our own self, in the quiet chamber within, and gave personal counsel and suggestions, which changed our inner and outer lives forever.

An outstanding example in my mind that Yeshua was beyond the ordinary man is that one morning, he sent me on an errand to carry vegetables, herbs and goat cheese to a bed-bound woman. I had left him behind teaching and hurried along the road, fussing in my head about how I would ever accomplish my other duties of serving the day's guests.

Suddenly, there was the Master standing at a bend in the road before me. What? I thought that I had just left him! I was so surprised. Smiling, he spoke to me, "Why worry so much? You're doing what I asked you to do and you're doing it well. This world is not created to be perfect, ever, no matter how hard we try. It's designed to be an on-going school. But see, you are seeking Oneness with God and Completeness in God and that's very good! *Always remember that nothing is lost in Spirit!* Every effort counts toward your final liberation and graduation from this School of Life!"

He warmly inquired of my parents and carried my basket for a while. He asked me if I was satisfied with my spiritual and meditative life and he thanked me for all my efforts both in meditation and service to others and he explained to me once again, "It all counts. Your efforts help you to evolve more quickly and your efforts help you and the whole world because we are all connected."

And then as suddenly as he had arrived in front of me, he was gone! [11]

Other examples abound of his ability to be in two places at once! To a child who couldn't travel to see him to be healed, Yeshua came to her in her home and healed her on a Sabbath day when he was still with us, teaching all day long and far into the night. Also, there was the family who prayed to him personally and to the One God to please help them now! Their house was burning down! He suddenly appeared next to them and put out the flames by commanding them to cease! [12]
His calming the flames of the fire was like when he calmed the wind and waves in a storm on the Sea of Galilee!

Although we were dumbfounded and truly incredulous, he told us that one day we too would be able to do all the things that he did, when we earned our own Christ-consciousness and had the faith the size of a mustard seed.

He said, "Truly I say to you, if you have faith as a grain of mustard seed, you will say to this mountain, 'Move from here to there,' and it will move. And nothing will be impossible for you." - Matthew 17:20 and Matthew 13:31-32

Well then, we were even more perplexed, wondering when our faith would be the size of a mustard seed! But perhaps it is more about its growth potential!

Oh, what joy! We were all content to follow him anywhere he led us and learn all we could learn. Being in his presence made us believe that as he had told us, "With God all things are possible!" - Matthew 19:26

And when he sent his disciples and some seventy others to teach and heal in other countries, they returned with reports that they indeed had been able to heal others!

"The seventy returned with joy, saying, "Lord, even the demons are subject to us through Your name." Luke 10:17

So, we continued to do our best in all ways and to love one another as he had taught us.

## Chapter 10:

## Lessons in How to Receive a Healing

One particularly dry, hot day, there were lines of people waiting to be healed by Yeshua. When the sun reached its zenith, a few who could no longer tolerate the blazing heat and the waiting any longer, stepped forward, stating they were cousins of Yeshua and had a right to see him first.

As they reached the calm, powerful face of Yeshua, they were silenced outwardly and inwardly. He spoke, "I would love to heal you, but first it requires your proper attitude! Today you have been impatient and unkind to step ahead of your neighbors. I am sorry that I can only heal you as much as you deserve. Sit down here and calm yourselves. Watch the beautiful and receptive faces of these dear ones and you may learn some humility and gratitude." [13]

Over the long hours, as they watched both the Master and the endless injured and sick, their hearts were transformed.

Yeshua then turned to them and said, "You may indeed be distant cousins of mine, but you have no more rights to my time and attention than anyone else. We are all equals in the sight of the One God."

They were sincerely penitent and grateful, and he did heal them. Yeshua added a warning that they must maintain their new attitudes of gratitude, humility and patience or their maladies would return in greater force; it was simply the divine law. "Remember, love your neighbor as you love yourself." - Luke 10:27

Not everyone could receive what Yeshua had to give them of healing, forgiveness, and a divine life of truth and inner freedom. Some examples were that sometimes their thoughts of anger and revenge over the death of a loved one got in the way or they were attached to their current rigid beliefs or their bad habits. When he wanted to help and couldn't, a look of great sadness shown on the dear Master's face. He knew that their soul would have to wait even longer until they could be receptive and open to his truths and his great, healing light. At times, he was still able to heal them, but if they did not change their misguided ways, the malady returned! He even forewarned them but still they were unable to change. He predicted, however, that sooner or later, all souls will return to the One God of love and bliss because that is our destiny and we are all children of God, without exception.

Later, that same long day, Yeshua expressed his need for rest and food and meditation. However, as we were preparing our camp and the night's meal, a stranger called to him from the bushes, "Master, I have been waiting all day. I didn't want to frighten anyone. I am a leper. Can you help me?"

I was filled with consternation and protectiveness for Yeshua's peace and recuperation, but Yeshua suddenly leapt to his feet, crying with such great love,

"Oh, my neighbor is here!" His love for people always gave him more energy.

Yeshua healed him with one giant embrace. For a brief moment, before I could react, I saw that the leprosy was present in the body of Yeshua and then just as suddenly it was gone! [14]

The man was thrilled and grateful, of course, but told of his family also suffering. They all appeared from behind the bushes also, missing noses and ears and fingers. Yeshua had them sit around the fire and had them imagine its warmth to be the love of God healing them. This time I saw no mark or disfigurement appeared on the body of Yeshua. [14]

Soon there were shouts of joy and thanksgiving and laughter, but the Master quieted them and bade them go within and thank the Father in silence.

We all feasted that night together, as neighbors and

friends, and got to know one another. We laughed knowing that these dear people now vibrant with health could have their former lives back with more love and appreciation for God and His Goodness than ever before! Such joy we felt! Oh, I wished that all people could sit with Yeshua in this informal way and experience this joy of divine fellowship!

# Chapter 11:

## *All Creatures Respond to Love*

People were not the only ones of God's creations who were drawn by Yeshua's endless love. Animals were often healed of ailments and injuries also. He loved them deeply for their innocence and how they reflected the will of God so easily and perfectly. We, unlike the animals, have free will.[15] However, we do not often reflect God's will, until we are shown the why and how by a true Master.

I remember one time when the Master healed both a family of goats and their owner at the same time. The owner had been beating them because of the poor quality of their milk. The poor milk was affecting his earnings and his lifestyle so in his frustration, he decided that beating them would at least relieve his frustration and might even encourage them to make better milk. Of course, it made matters worse. The goats became ill and produced less milk. In the process of beating them, the man had injured his wrist. Instant karma, I thought in my righteous anger. In contrast, Yeshua talked to the man and reasoned with him to try something new and thank the goats every morning for the milk they provided, no matter how scant the milk might be. As he agreed and they clasped hands and wrists. Yeshua's powerful vibration of love healed the man's wrist. I hope that the man tried the gratitude technique on his goats. He certainly had an amazing demonstration of the power of love, if he could receive it. And, I'm certain that Yeshua blessed the goats' health as well!

One foggy morning before the sun rose, I awoke to glance toward Yeshua. I saw his usual upright form meditating but also shapes and shadows around him. Because of the usual deep peace that permeated the area when he meditated, I was not fearful but startled and sat up to see more clearly. What was I seeing? As my eyes adjusted, I could see first two antelope with very long horns and some very large birds sitting in a branch above his head, some owls, raptors, hawks, even a vulture. Around him were some deer, sheep, goats and what?!... a snake had wrapped himself around Yeshua's neck! Also, a pack of wolves sat quietly and respectfully at his feet. All these animals were not bothering one another and did not even seem to care about the others. Their only focus was Yeshua, drawn by his powerful vibration, no doubt, of love, appreciation and peace. Yeshua stirred perhaps with awareness of me and the wolves rolled over on their backs, just like dogs, to be petted. As Yeshua stood, he stroked the snake also and he gently slid away.

What a sight!

## Chapter 12:

## The Early Morning Surprise

One unusually still and beautiful morning, we woke to the sound of laughter ~ Yeshua laughing loudly, deeply, joyously. The birds started to chatter and suddenly rose in mass, as if they could not hold all the joy emanating from him, high into the sky and then returning to land all around him. We were accustomed to the habit of sitting up to meditate with him as soon as we woke but this way of waking was to be relished, cherished and even emulated, at least in thought.

Yeshua kept laughing so fully and freely that we all began to laugh, huge belly laughs right along with him. After the laughter calmed from joyous rollicking waves into comfortable wavelets of mirth-beyond-words, we just naturally and easily meditated with him, enjoying the soft vibrant bliss, deep and still within. [16]

We recognized that bliss as so familiar, even though it was new to us, at least in this life. That ever-new bliss was our own joyous nature and oneness with the All. It was delectable!

He later explained that he had been communing with Our Heavenly Father in the form of his Guru. Guru is another word for divine or spiritual teacher. The Guru teaches us how to find God within and become masters of our own self.

He said that in a past life his guru [17] had been called Elijah, when Yeshua was Elisha. And, in this life, Elijah came to be Yeshua's supporter as John the Baptist.

He was beholding in his meditation, the story of life like moving-pictures, [18] showing that this life is created not to harm us, but to teach us and prod us to return to our joyful, natural state of the consciousness of God's Ever-New and Ever-existing Bliss.

He told us that he saw past, present and future all-at-once because in God there is no time and that in Truth, we are already free and illumined and one with God, all people and all nature. In this consciousness there is no sadness, no temporary happiness; there are no friends, no enemies; all is One and we are One!

Serving the people that day was easy and joyful. We served with limitless energy. We came to understand from our own experience of this endless energy how Yeshua is able to serve so long and so joyously, with this full awareness of ever-new Bliss and Joy sustaining him.

Oh, we loved and appreciated him so much!

## Chapter 13:

## *Intimate Moments with My Master*

It was so very rare; well, it just never happened before, to just get a chance to ask my master private questions but here we were together and alone.

Can mankind really change? I asked him.

Yeshua answered,

"Well, we have seen it in individuals who come here to listen and walk away changed in their attitudes. But on a larger scale, we are planting seeds that will grow in time. Change is not usually instantaneous unless the person has made efforts to change and improve in past lives."

Why not just show your glory like you did to some of the disciples on the mountain? Perhaps you could demonstrate your glory just one day per year?

He answered, "There are people, especially the Zealots, who would love to force me into such a bold assertion, but they are not in tune with God's law of man's free will and God's attracting love for us all. God wants us to come to Him freely, through love alone."

"Such a demonstration would only cause war, bloodshed, disbelief and confusion. The quiet way seems slower but is actually faster in the long run."

"Our Father already shows his glory in various and regular ways. He sends great souls to earth frequently. He sends great and varied shows of beauty in nature. He expresses His love for us through the love of our parents. He often answers our prayers.[19]　　　　But these graces are subtle and personal, given to the individual as that person earns and deserves them and as he can benefit from them."

"God can't force us to be good or accept his glory. He has given us free will and will never take it back. I must follow His Will. I want to do so."

Why can't I remember past lives? I just get little glimpses.

"The Heavenly Father is actually protecting you from the grief of a memory of having injured someone in the past or from having a pride that you did something noble and grand or talented. He wants you to have a fresh start every time. He does what He does, always from Divine Love. He is Love."

"A fully awakened spine, brain and soul are earned. When we are fully awake in God, we will remember our true identity in Spirit as children of God; we will remember everything from past lives and we will know our future as well."

Why do people die young, like my husband?

"It was so painful for you, wasn't it? We get so attached and you are still angry about it, I see. Well, surrender and faith are good ways to heal. Let go of this wonderful soul as much as you can. Keep giving him to the Father of Supreme Love as many times a day as it takes."

"Trust that he is well and happy in his new divine life, in his new spiritual body of light, that he is growing exactly as he should. He still loves you but has a greater understanding of it all and what a great drama this all is. The funny thing is that we all agreed to come here and play our parts in the drama!"

"And the fact that he was killed by a Roman complicates things still further, doesn't it? Forgiveness is required. Forgive him for thinking that force can win. Forgive the Roman for his feelings of superiority. They both made the same mistake that thinking force is superior and can win and make them happy.[20]

"For all those who take up the sword will perish by the sword. - Matthew 26:52

So have compassion for them all. And, forgive yourself for your part too."

What is forgiveness, Master? Is true forgiveness even possible for a regular person? And why do bad things happen to good people and good things happen to bad people?"

"Forgiveness is unconditional love.[21]
It begins with knowing that you are the soul; you are not just your personality. The reason for this life is to teach us what we need to learn. The personality may be hurt but that personality is not your soul, which is never hurt. Remember what I have asked of you all, to keep forgiving.
"Forgive your enemy not just until seven times but forgive seventy times seven!" - Matthew 18:22

"We are here for just a short time to learn something that God has given us to learn. We can forgive others because we know that we too have made horrible mistakes in this life and in our past lives, which require forgiveness too. A regular person can forgive with the help of God and His great, divine detachment."

"This earth is created to teach us that we are just visitors here, not permanent residents. Anyone who injures and anyone who is injured are here to realize that only the sharing of love gives permanent happiness and freedom. Revenge can never make us happy, neither can trying to teach the other a lesson by hurting him back."

"It may be helpful to see the person who needs forgiveness as just a little child who didn't know better, who thought by his actions that he could be happy."

"Both good and bad happen to all people. In the end, we all reap what we have sown by our actions. It may take a lifetime or more. It only appears that a bad person is rewarded because his or her bad actions will indeed one day be returned, just like a boomerang!"

"And good people may suffer terribly but it is only a temporary, although a grueling experience. After full effort to rid himself of his malady, if a person surrenders to God as fully as possible and tries to keep a positive attitude, then that suffering can become a proof of his or her unconditional love for God. His reward in the heavenly realms will be great!"

What about the animals, will they progress also like people do? Some of my animals have been really smart and loving and one even saved my life!

"Yes, I know and yes, they do progress. What they do with mostly with instinct and attunement with the Divine Will must also be accomplished with complete free will. And yes, you will see them again! Pray for them and send them your love and thanks and appreciation. Pray that they progress quickly on their own path to full Spiritual Realization."

Master, are you the Messiah that was prophesied in the Torah?

"I am He. I am not a military leader who will lead the Jewish people to their independence."

"I am He who teaches how to gain inner soul freedom to anyone and everyone who is willing to follow my example and do the inner work. In this way of prayer and meditation, we can gain inner, lasting freedom and joy."

"I bring a new testament or covenant that replaces the old covenant of anger and revenge with forgiveness and love, a great love that grows from Divine Contact Within. Only with Divine Love can we all become truly happy, blissful sons and daughters of God."

Master, it is so hard to meditate when there are Roman soldiers around every corner and my neighbors are deprived of their work or jailed or sick or worse!

"Yes, I know but just do your best each day. A little

meditation is better than no meditation. Do not give-in to the temptation that you will wait to meditate until circumstances are more perfect. They will never be perfect. Get up before dawn, if necessary. Remember you are earning your spiritual liberation. You are earning your way out of here! All your meditations, all your prayers, all your sacrifices – they all count! You can live in a land of light when you die and never return here, unless you want to return to help others. You must fight for your time with God. Once you are in the meditation posture, relax as much as possible. Trust God and trust me to guide you also."

"And feel encouraged too, that when you are struggling the most, you are often spiritually progressing the most! Know that the Heavenly Father sees and knows all."

"Again, I say: everything you do for God, your love and faith in me and in your inner Self, your love for others, your sacrifices, your meditations, your willingness and efforts to do right. It all counts! Remember, nothing is lost in Spirit!"

Will you stay with me always Master? I am so tired of my loved ones dying.

"Yes, be assured. I am with you until the end of the ages. Call upon me anytime. I want us to be the best and most intimate of friends. Trust in me. Trust that whatever experiences that I send you, good or bad, are for your highest good and for your quickest release into the beauty and bliss of God's ultimate freedom in Him. I love you always, most beautiful soul!"

To end our conversation, Yeshua added:

*"Everything that interests you, every detail of your life, tell me about it. I'll listen with such attention and joy. If you only knew. Tell others to act with Me as they would with the Intimate Friend who knows all the secrets of their hearts."* [22]

# Chapter 14:

## Yeshua's Trip to India

*Yeshua told us of his youth and these are some of the highlights that I remember, plus others that were told to me by other disciples of Yeshua:*

It was the custom for Jewish families, at the time of a child's youth, to propose marriage arrangements. Yeshua was a popular choice among parents in Nazareth both for his skill in carpentry and for his magnetic and pleasing personality. However, Yeshua, at thirteen or any age, had no interest in marriage arrangements. He only honored his commitment to His Divine Father, the One God.

Yeshua told his parents that it was God's will for him to return the visit of the three Wise Men who had visited him at his birth. He asked for their blessing. He would take the trade route going east and spend time learning from each of the Wise Men. Mary understood and agreed; she already trusted his judgment and attunement with God. Joseph knew that he had reached the limit of what he could teach Yeshua and he knew that the Jewish schools were too limited for him; Yeshua was already teaching the teachers! Mary and Joseph believed that God would guard the safety of their divine son when the right time came, and he was older. However, Yeshua believed the right time was right then, that it was his spiritual destiny to go immediately. So, to spare his dearly loved parents, he left in the night.

Yeshua began his journey by walking south and then north along the Sea of Tiberius or Galilee. His first goal was to reach Damascus and the silk trade route. Whenever opportunity offered itself, he would travel for a while with a family who took him in. He loved the Sea of Galilee and Capernaum and intuited that one day he would meet some dear friends in that region who would support him in his Mission. After some weeks, he arrived at the trade route where silk, spices, gold, silver and other valuable cargo was carried west to the Mediterranean Sea and then on to countries farther west, south and north.

A camel caravan going east to India agreed to take Yeshua, if he would care for their camels. The camels loved him instantly and he loved them. Their owners were surprised to see them so obedient to him, even after long days of work. They also noted that over the long months of travel, the camels never got ill either.

This was a most carefree and exciting part of young Yeshua's life. He felt that he was finally getting closer to his Divine destiny; he longed to be of service to others in a greater way, much greater. After the days' travels, he told stories of adventure and courage to the children on the caravan and talked with the adults of his beliefs in the One God of Love that lives within us all. He also shared his beliefs with the villagers along the way, encouraging them to live lives of honesty, truth and compassion for all and that they would be blessed in return.

Many months of travel later, the caravan was nearing India and a messenger arrived with the news that King Balthazar was expecting him. Immediately, in eager anticipation and against his companions' loving objections, Yeshua left with the same messenger, expressing his thanks, love and eternal friendship to all.

When Yeshua and Balthazar met, the joy was palpable in the air. This was not an older man greeting a young man but two advanced souls, two soul friends meeting after a long absence, as if it were lifetimes.

They were in fact dear, dear friends from many past lives together. Balthazar was a king of kings, so noble, beautiful, loving. He was a true saint and lover of God. He had known by Divine attunement that Yeshua was coming and had prepared an elegant welcome for him with music, dancing, reminiscences and meditation on the One God of Love and Spirit.

Yeshua stayed several years with Balthazar, [23]

learning all he could from him of spiritual principles, cosmic realities, various methods of spiritual healing and kriya yoga meditation. They frequently meditated for long hours and sometimes they fasted and meditated for days and weeks. They shared a vision of a future world of peace and prosperity and Divine-attunement.

Finally, they both knew the time was right for Yeshua to travel south in India, near the Persian empire to meet Melchior. Balthazar sent Melchior a message by pigeon about Yeshua's arrival in a few months.

Arriving after dark, the meeting with Melchior[24] was a quiet event. Joyfully they prayed and meditated together in great inner bliss, under the vast and brilliant stars.

Melchior expressed his saintliness with a deep and serious nature and with him Yeshua discussed and planned the best way he could fulfill his mission and what possible spiritual practices he could leave after his death to support and inspire the people in the coming centuries. Most people were not ready to learn kriya yoga meditation because they did not understand energy or thought or visualization yet.

They discussed the huge, God-ordained sacrifice that would require the utmost love and tranquility and attunement with God. Ages ago, in the vast halls of eternity, Yeshua had agreed to this task with His Father God because such a sacrifice, made in true love, would change the hearts of humanity and speed their spiritual evolution toward their true divinity. However, under God's law of free choice, it was understood that Yeshua could still say no at any time to this greatest of sacrifices of his own life. Times were dark and people were still entrenched in their thought-habit of murder and revenge.

If Yeshua agreed to do the will of His Heavenly Father in that final hour, they both believed that it would change and uplift the hearts of all seeking men and women through the centuries who would be infinitely inspired by his loving sacrifice, his teachings of love and forgiveness and his overcoming of the last enemy, death.

The time came for Yeshua to begin sharing with others in a much greater and more public way. He knew it was time for him to combine all he already intuitively knew with the new revelations of truth he had recently realized into his own way of serving the One God in all. He would teach, share the great truths of love and forgiveness, and heal the people that he met along his way to meet Gaspar. [25]

Of the three Wise Men, Gaspar served the now adult Yeshua in a most practical and helpful way as he began his ministry. Gaspar helped him deepen his detachment and calmness in the face of conflicting values and severe political and religious criticism and condemnation as he encountered various sects of India and their practices. With some religions, Yeshua was in complete attunement and shared their values. With others, he had to refute their religious practices because their traditions had become greater in importance than God Himself. He offered gentle and wise correction, when possible.

Yeshua was able to talk with Gaspar and compare their Divine and intuitive understanding about how his teachings would be received by the masses.

In healing others, Yeshua learned temperance and when to hold back on healing someone when they, as souls, would learn more by keeping their particular malady or challenge. He had to intuit and know what their stage of spiritual development was in order to help them most. At other times, Gaspar offered suggestions on how to balance his openness and endless compassion for others with firmness, greater wisdom and divine timing.

It was not that the three wise men were greater in God-realization or wisdom than Yeshua. It was their wisdom and compassion and attunement with the One God of Love that was helpful and stabilizing. Just like his revered parents, Mary and Joseph, who were already God-realized and were able to help, inspire and guide young Yeshua in their unique and God-ordained ways. In truth, each one of us will eventually, in our God-realized

Divine state of awareness, be able to impart certain facets of the uniqueness and power of God.

With each of the three Wise Men,[26] Yeshua meditated deeply and was able to absorb their singular God-realization or God-consciousness and enter into what each felt to be their favored aspect of the Infinite God. Divine answers came not by debate or words but through the deep and wordless meditations that they shared together.

Yeshua's travels took him through many Hindu cities of India – south to Calicut in Kerala, east to Puri on the Bay of Bengal and north to a Hemis Buddhist monastery in Ladakh, Nepal [27]                and he spent some years with the monotheistic Sakya Buddhist sect near Nepal and Tibet. Everywhere he went he shared the truths of the One God of love, forgiveness, and serving God in others. He was called Saint Isa and was highly revered. To the receptive, he was an incarnation of love, beauty, simplicity, and peace.

In Ladakh, Yeshua began to realize that the optimum time was approaching for his return home and he began his journey, reversing his steps to go to the homes of each of the three Wise Men, his dear and revered friends and guides.

At his last stop at Balthazar's home, he found that the

three Wise Men and many of his friends had all gathered together again for one more visit with him. They revered him with an unspeakable reverence, calling him as they always had: the Christ, the Messiah, the Savior of Mankind, the Son of the Living God.

They all gave him their unconditional love and blessings and promised their continuing prayers for his great Mission to be fully successful with the blessings of the One God of Love.

*And that is all that I know of those years of Yeshua's trip to India as a youth and young man.*

## Chapter 15:

## Continual Blessings and Healings

We saw so many visible healings. Many people walked again, talked again, and could hear the beauty of voices and birdsong and music again. Lepers and those with all kinds of physical ailments were able to live happy and productive lives again. I'm guessing sometimes there would be 50 to over 100 healings in one day. The responses of those healed varied according to individual temperament and personality. Some people acted as if they deserved it, that naturally Yeshua should heal them. Others were very grateful and gracious and praised the One God and Yeshua. Some were embarrassed, as if they knew why they got the infirmity in the first place! Others were so stunned that they could say nothing but look at Yeshua or a family member. But almost always, there was surprise and joy and praise and gratitude to God!

Yeshua would even heal the animals that the people brought to him. And, I suspect that he silently healed the animals, even as he walked through the villages. I feel this to be true because of the delighted animal voices of all kinds as he passed. Sometimes they bounced up and down. What a joy to see and to hear them!

There were the dramatic healings by God through Yeshua that most of us had heard about but had not seen:

Water was transformed into excellent wine at a marriage feast

Flames of a raging fire about to consume a family home were calmed by speaking to the flames [28]

Yeshua stopped a storm at sea to save his disciples, just by raising his arms and speaking to the wind.

Yeshua walked on top of the Sea of Galilee.

A woman was healed of years of bleeding just by touching Yeshua's robe.

All these miracles were so powerful and beautiful!

However, perhaps the most interesting healings were the quiet, delayed healings. Of course, I rarely saw the result of those healings but Yeshua cared even more about people's souls than their bodies. It was as if he was deeply speaking to their souls and that alone was a miracle. His love was endless and deeply sincere. It was amazing to watch him day after day, week after week, month after month serving everyone he met with the exact love or gentle correction or healing that they most needed.

To one man he said, "If you will be strong and resist drinking until the third Sabbath day passes, you will lose all desire to drink too much wine." He wanted him to develop strength and patience and will power. He encouraged the man, "Focus on helping others."

To an ill young woman very desirous of getting married, he counseled,

"You are compensating for bad actions of a former life with this illness. If you can patiently endure your troubles for another year, all your symptoms will subside and not return. You will also attract a better husband in this way. He will be attracted to your real inner beauty and not just your body's beauty."
She also felt encouraged by Yeshua to endure and wait.

Sometimes he didn't heal people at all. To a beautiful blind lady, Yeshua said, "I'm sure that if you wish it, God will heal you right now but if you will continue as you are now and stay as cheerful and devoted as you are today, you will advance very far spiritually in this one life." She chose to stay blind. He encouraged her to speak her truth of the One God and His kindness and to continue her singing to Him. Yeshua encouraged her, "You will be able to help and inspire many!" [29]

There were deep healings of clinging and difficult emotions, like my own dark emotions, like hatred and revenge, especially toward the Romans. My hot anger was gradually replaced with greater and greater forgiveness and greater compassion and understanding. Great and overwhelming grief and sadness for murders and the sudden loss of loved ones were eased. Yeshua gave many joyful reassurances of what their loved ones were doing in heaven or the astral. In some instances, he told them that their loved ones had already been reborn, sometimes even into their own families, explaining the deep love they instantly felt for them and why their children had such similar characteristics to their lost loved ones.

Sometimes although people were full of faith and receptive and were living perfect lives in tune with God, they still had some malady that would not go away. In these cases, although it appeared unfair, the Master recommended that they see the malady through to its end and burn off the results of a long-forgotten action or pattern from a past life and to remember that sometimes our loving Father God is actually protecting us from an even worse malady or fate. Bolstered by his loving encouragement, they agreed to do their best.

The deepest healings he gave us were for our souls. He loved us deeply and his greatest desire was that we be free of the desires and demands of the little self, so we could be free in our True Self of Spirit. His most fervent wish was for us to love the One God and put Him first before all other desires, even before the good desires.

He wanted us to take time for prayer and meditation each morning and before bed as our primary and sustaining spiritual food.  In so doing, all our emotional worries and concerns would melt away in the Divine contact, in the great inner stillness that he had often shown us, so full of deep peace, contentment and joy.

What a joy Yeshua had given me in asking me to spend the year following him. That blessing alone would be all I would ever need. Nevertheless, I knew it would be difficult to leave His blessed company.

## Chapter 16:

## Jazbot Celebration!

We had never heard of such a celebration as Jazbot but it became clear to us when Yeshua explained that it was a way of celebrating our love and friendship for each other.

He had sent us all on errands and when we returned in the evening, he had a large crackling fire going and fresh flowers, fruit and sweetmeats which were very new and foreign to us.

We sat around him at random, so we thought, but each setting had a special individual present for each one wrapped in beautiful multi-colored cloth.

He spoke to us of the power of love, loyalty and friendship and how friendship is the highest relationship, just below in importance to our relationship with God! [30]

"You, my beloved friends, are treasures to me! I treasure our intimate friendship and the trust we share. It sustains me. I will be your friend for eternity, through all your incarnations, both on earth and in heaven."

"This is Jazbot when we give special gifts, based on our true understanding of our friends' natures, skills, interests and needs. I first celebrated Jazbot in India with friends there and I think it is a wonderful way to show love. Today I am the giver but in future, when I am gone, you can support and share with one another in this way too."

"I give you these gifts as a symbol of the highest and best gift: my promise to introduce each of you to the Father! I will do this one day when your work is finished."

Then, we began the opening of gifts one by one. Each gift was accompanied by his precious spoken words of appreciation and encouragement for our spiritual journey and for following his teachings.

My gift was one that I didn't understand at first – a little doll, just a small one to hold in my hand, but she was beautiful and the more I looked at her, the more . . . I remembered! I had lived one past life as a mother to a very similar-looking child and in other lives too, I had many sons and daughters and was happily married to many long-lived spouses. A deep satisfaction entered my heart as these memories revealed themselves.

Other memories of past lives dedicated to meditation entered my heart with the encouragement that I could indeed meditate that deeply and well again! I had succeeded before and would do so again!

Other gifts that disciples received were from his travels in the East. They included the following: unique planting seeds, books, artwork, a plain-looking rock with sparkling crystals inside, special spices for cooking, medicinal herbs, a necklace with a Sanskrit symbol for God, special sandals, a song book, sacred texts, lovely shawls of various colors and fabrics, goblets, and toys.

We were all deeply touched. I wondered what inner vistas or memories of past lives his gifts opened for them . . . Such an outward show of affection and appreciation none of us had ever expected or even dimly imagined!

Our Jazbot celebration ended with singing some songs and some people danced. Then we went our separate ways to meditate, carrying our gifts and deep thanks for a Master who knew us all so intimately and so well and so generously served us as if we were each his most beloved friend of all!

As he once told us, "The Guru is the best of Givers!" This means that only the Guru, the advanced Spiritual Teacher, such as Yeshua who knows God intimately can introduce us to God and God's Bliss Consciousness. [31]

He has promised that he would! Just the thought of it, the privilege of it, dove my consciousness into a deep meditation.

## Chapter 17:

## The Return of Mary

One day there was special laughter and warmth in the camp where we were. Mary, the mother of Yeshua, had joined us again.

The entire day was spent in stories about the disciples' adventures and the healings that Yeshua performed and that they also had been able to perform, through God's blessing.

When Yeshua was busy with others and when Mary was alone again at last, I plucked up the courage to ask her about Yeshua's birth. She said that she thought about this event often and was most happy to share it with me.

Mary said that during those final days of her pregnancy, they took the trip from Nazareth to Bethlehem for the census. Although the trip was very long on the only donkey that they had, she never felt fatigued. And during the actual process of delivery, she never felt worried or afraid. She said it was deeply peaceful and utterly pain-free! For her, she beamed, it was one of his first miracles. She felt to be in a state of grace the entire time.

"Barely had baby Yeshua been born, when he had visitors." She explained, "So, from the very first moments, we had to share him with the world. Everyone seemed to know that he had arrived, and some shepherds came first, carrying milk and cheese, a ewe and small lamb as gifts and of course they brought their devotion, bowing with awe. They were entranced by the smiling baby Yeshua, with his soft loving eyes that took everyone in."

She continued sharing, "Everyone seemed to easily kneel before him, because we all felt an unspeakable reverence with no reservations. Everyone wanted to get close to the great love coming from his eyes! Even the animals responded to his love with their attentive quietness. The night seemed unusually bright, fragrant, joyous and full of love."

"The shepherds told us that a host of angels had visited them in the fields and lit up the sky with their brightness and their singing."

"And an angel said unto them, Fear not: for, behold, I bring you good tidings of great joy, which will be to all people. For unto you is born this day in the city of David a savior who is Christ the Lord. And this will be a sign for you: you will find the babe wrapped in swaddling clothes and lying in a manger." - Luke 2:10 – 12

"And suddenly there was with the angel a multitude of the heavenly host praising God, and saying, 'Glory to God in the highest, and on earth peace, good will toward men." -- Luke 2:13-14

"… and so the shepherds went looking for him and found him right there in the stable where we were. Can you imagine?"

"And later", Mary said, "some wealthy kings came to see him. They were wise men from the East. They called Yeshua the Christ and the Messiah and the son of the Living God and Isha which means Lord!"

"All of these visits added to Joseph's and my own belief in him, that indeed he is the son of God. I do not mean son in an exclusive sense", she said, "because we are all children of God. [32]         Son of God means that he is among the first of God's children to make it all the way to Christ-consciousness; certainly he is the first among us!"

What could I even say to that remarkable story but, since I felt so at ease, I asked another personal question: "Why don't you stay with us, Mary?"

She answered me, "It is not my son's wish that I do so. He says that I can better serve him and our Father God by meditating at home and praying for him and all those who come to him. He also knows how attached I am to him and he wants me to be attached to God Alone. This will make it a bit easier for me when the final day comes."

When I asked what that meant, she would not answer. I knew that I had reached my limit of questions, but how uplifting and fabulous her answers had been! I wondered if one person could be more blessed than me.

## Chapter 18:

## Returning Home

Yeshua didn't exactly say, "Go now." I just knew it was time. We would be passing near my village again soon. So, I asked him directly, "Is it time for me to return home, Master?" and he replied,

"We have loved having you with us! You have the heart of service and you have always kept up on your meditations. I thank you so much for looking after the children and their mothers! Go now and teach what you have learned in your own village and those villages near your own. Especially I want you to teach the children. You have a special way with children, of helping them to understand. The One God will be with you and will guide you. I will be with you also, always! Believe this truth, no matter what happens."

"Go in peace!"

As I walked the gravel path back to my little village, I squeezed the little ball in my pocket and I discovered that all the longings of my heart for love, for a family and children had been dissolved into a much greater love and longing to serve the One God, my Master Yeshua and all the children of the world.

# Chapter 19:

## *Arriving to True Home*

Well, my optimism and faith were immediately put to the test because at the door of our home, I found that father was sick. At the sight of him, I longed to run for Yeshua to come and heal him, but my father wouldn't let me leave him again. I also knew and feared that if I did, I would never see him again. Father was just happy to see me and very calm and content that it was his time to leave for home in the One God. Despite my urgent prayers and diligent care, he died soon after my return home. I had to just accept it. I consoled myself that at least I had been able to see him one more time.

However, mother soon became ill too. I nursed her for many months, applying the best methods of healing that I knew with the prayerful expectancy that Yeshua had taught us. I taught mother all I had learned but my dear angelic mother died too. Her death came almost simultaneously with receiving the unbelievable news of the cruel and unjust trial and crucifixion of Yeshua.

It was unthinkable. I merely went through the motions of a burial for my mother and normal duties of life. With the deaths of all three of my loved ones, plus now Yeshua, I was in complete shock. Then as some awareness of the facts returned, I sank into a deep depression. My feeble efforts to meditate yielded no peace or satisfaction. Weeks of emotional and mental torture passed. I cried out my agonies and anger and contempt for our enemies to the One God.

How could You allow this to happen to the dearest person of all? He didn't deserve it. The Romans are scum! The Sanhedrin are bullying manipulators!

You were so powerful, Yeshua, why didn't you protect yourself? I love you so much. Why did you leave?

Then I felt alternatingly guilty. Had I learned nothing about the love and forgiveness that Yeshua had taught us, that the kingdom of God is within us?

My anger, hurt and confusion received no reconciliation but then I began to hear conflicting news. Some said that Yeshua was not dead at all, that he had appeared to his disciples and to the women!

It was all so confusing! One day, in a secluded garden near our village, I forced myself to meditate and focus on the Goodness and Love of God... I tried visualizing his face . . . and suddenly there he was, right in front of me!

"Master!" A deluge of tears and sobs and groans

flooded his feet, as I alternately looked up through blurred vision at his kind, loving shining eyes.

As I couldn't yet rise, he knelt to my level and lifted me to stand.

"Oh Master, how could people be so mistaken? They said that you were crucified!"

"Well, they are correct. I was crucified and died. It was quite complete! But God had a wondrous plan, that if I was willing to die in such a horrible way, it would demonstrate what true, unconditional love looks like, love without any limit!" [33]

"Then, because of that great Divine Love, I resurrected this body, of course with God's help and my Master's help."
"...I laid down my life...no man taketh it from me, but I lay it down of myself. I have the power to lay it down, and I have power to take it again." – John 10:17-18

One day, as children of God, you will all learn to do this and know that we can take up the body or put it down anytime we wish!"
"Verily, verily, I say unto you, he that believeth on me, the works that I do, shall he do also; and greater works than these shall he do; because I go unto my Father." – John 14:12

"Your parents were both ready to go. They lived

very good lives and are safe and very happy now. And, believe it or not, your husband was ready to go too. They all needed to move on to greater fields of challenge and growth! Have no worries or regrets about them!"

"I am here! See my scars? I am truly your Yeshua. There has been no loss. It was all a gift for you all because of my love for you and because of the Heavenly Father's greater Love."

"So, stop grieving and pitying yourself! It is time to go teach, as I asked you to do. First, let's sit and meditate together."

It was easy to meditate with Yeshua at my side. Suddenly, I heard a great roaring sound but not really a physical sound; it completely filled and comforted my whole being. I felt very large, like one with the whole of humanity and all space. This great, roaring stillness was expansive and so comforting and lasted an eternity, it seemed. I now call it ever-new joy or bliss!

As I came to normal awareness, I found that I was completely recovered from any delusions of sadness. Yeshua explained, "This is the Comforter that I promised to send you all." - John 14:26

"The Comforter [34]                    is the vibration of God in creation, the great Om, Aum, Amen. Amin. From now on, when you prayerfully sit perfectly still to meditate, eyes raised gently to focus on God, you will hear and feel God's great Sound of Om. It is my gift to you, to all people, when they tune-in with Spirit."

"Teach. "The Comforter, which is the Holy Ghost, whom the Father sends in my name, shall teach you all things and bring all things to your remembrance, whatsoever I have said unto you." - John 14:26

My words will be more clear and understandable than when you first heard them. The Comforter will guide you as you share with others. I will guide you."

"Be at peace, my beloved one! Live in God's great Joy!"

"Peace I leave with you, my peace I give unto you, not as the world giveth, give I unto you. Let not your heart be troubled, neither let it be afraid." – John 14:27

"Keep marching on and know that there is no loss. Know that I love and bless you always. You can call on me in Spirit anytime because I am with you always!"

I gazed on his beautiful form again, before it gradually faded from my sight into a gentle, golden light.

## Chapter 20:

## *Memories of Meditating with the Master*

One of Yeshua's main purposes in life was to teach us how to go within and meditate on the One God as endless love, peace beyond understanding, and expanding joy. [35]

This contact within in meditation, he told us, would give us wisdom and the ability to live the truth of God's uplifting, sustaining and forgiving love.

"Practice right away in the morning before doing your duties. Make God first in your lives," he advised us.

Yeshua taught us to quiet our breathing and focus within, gently lifting the eyes toward the Spiritual Eye, the shining sun of God within the forehead. "Or," he said, "you may see it as a little white star, or you may see nothing at all. Everyone is different, so just be patient. The important part is keeping your eyes upturned. Gently and patiently push away and ignore the thoughts of the day. It is normal to go through the struggle with disruptive thoughts and memories but," he encouraged us, "keep trying and eventually your thoughts will obey you. Practice feeling God's peace."

Often, we would meditate with Yeshua in our camp or we would meditate in people's homes where we were invited. He would also take us with him to quiet places to pray and meditate. Mysteriously, on several occasions, when he took us away into nature, people would try to find us, searching for the Master for solace or healing. They could not find us! It was as if our deep stillness and silence and inner communion with God cast around us an invisible cloak. People would walk right past us, without seeing us. Another explanation might be that Yeshua had the power to redirect people's thoughts in a different direction and I'm sure that he sent them a silent blessing.

These times meditating with our Master were great treasures to us! They gave us strength and renewal. Yeshua would often speak to us of the importance of this inner contact with God.

He told us, "When I am gone from your sight, you will need this way of gaining strength. You will grieve for me and it will be harder to meditate but keep bringing the thought of me into your mind and heart and I will bring you peace."

And to his main disciples, he said, "You will be tempted to quit and to return to your previous way of life and your families. Resist this temptation with meditation. You are destined for great lives of service to God and humanity."

"Remember the food I told you that you didn't know about? You would not have understood before, but meditation is my food and will be yours. It is the light of

God sustaining us all."

These are the other reminders about meditation that I recall that Yeshua repeatedly emphasized:

"Choose a quiet, secluded place to meditate. However, don't let noise or location stop you from meditating on the One Beloved. Imagine that you are dead to the world. Leave your thoughts of the world outside, just like you leave your sandals at a door."

"Pray in this way: 'Just for this time when I am with You, my Beloved God, in prayer and meditation, I am dead to the world, to my family, to my possessions. Nothing matters to me except this time with You, my Beloved God. I have no attachments, no expectations. In this time of stillness with You, I am not asking for anything; I accept whatever You may choose to send me. It is such a blessing to be quiet and still in Your Presence, my Lord.'"

"Most importantly, dear ones, be still. Don't move. When you move about, your energy goes out into your arms and hands, your legs and feet, outward into action and more thoughts. Go inward. Be still and know God is within you."

"There is a reason to gently lift your eyes upward and keep them there because as you know, when they are open and looking straight out, they are focused on the world of men. And when your eyes go downward, you are most likely day-dreaming or sleeping."

"I have shown you the way of loving God and others from moment to moment. Fill your moments with thoughts of God and loving your neighbors and serving them. Pray for all, especially your enemies. When you do this during the day, your meditations will be easier."

"The fulfillment that you seek is within you. There within you is your kingdom of permanent happiness. Inner fullness of joy and bliss are there. Outside are tempting material pleasures that never last. Only God's peace and joy will last and be ever new. Although you can't see Him, just like you can't see the wind, He is right with you. I promise you that as you give time to this practice of meditation, inner peace and joy and love will come and it will get easier and easier and one day there it is – your own Christhood, Christ-consciousness and oneness with God."

"This will help you. Know that God is in you. He is breathing you. When you breathe, you breathe in God. When you breathe out, you breathe out God. He is everywhere. There is no place where God is not. He is digesting your food and pumping the blood in your heart and through you He is loving your friends and family. He is love itself, wisdom, light, joy, peace, calmness and power."

"You may think that you are alone and isolated when you meditate but, if you ask, a host of angels and saints will come to help you and I will come to help. Only the little self likes to think it is so very alone. Replace that thought that you are alone with the truth that we are all deeply loved by God as His Own. He is always with us."

"Meditation is more than just relaxation. Relaxation is a very important beginning but then, while relaxed, we must use our concentration to focus on the One God of Love."

"Consider which aspect of God will most inspire and motivate you to have a personal relationship with Spirit."

- "Who and what quality of God do you long and yearn for?
- Do you love the Father or Mother aspect of God?
- Do you think of God as Friend or Brother?
- Or, do you feel God as Infinite love, light, bliss, peace or as the sound of Aum, Amen, Amin?"

"Choose your favorite aspect of God and focus on that Manifestation. Having a Divine Focus will help your concentration in meditation and your practice of the Presence during the day. God is pleased to appear to you in the form that you most love!"

"You may ask, "What if I can't meditate at all sometimes?' or 'Why do I feel dry of devotion to God and unwilling to sit still?' Well, that happens to everyone who meditates. It is delusion or Satan, trying to dissuade and discourage us again. However, it is also a necessary part of the meditation path and makes you strong to resist and go on anyway. Just keep practicing the best you can. By lovingly continuing with your meditations, you learn to love God unconditionally because there is no visible reward; it teaches patience, perseverance and develops great inner strength."

"Remember, God responds to your every effort, every devotional call to Him; *nothing is ever lost in Spirit!*"

"Try to practice a little extra meditation each Shabbat, and more if possible, and you will progress highly in this life."

"Remember: all people are equal and have a soul which shines with the light of God. Nothing can erase or diminish that beauty and purity. Even when we make mistakes, even severe ones, our soul remains untouched and pure. We are all loved unconditionally. God is love and we are all parts of that Great Love, which makes us very special indeed."

"All churches who honor the One God are holy and sacred places. However, be warned that the practice of putting ritual first or the practice of talking too much can quickly become shallow and empty of love for God. Going within to stillness with love for the One God in meditation is best and all churches should learn it and teach it."

"Some people wish for powers when they meditate, like the power God gave me to heal. Meditate to love God Alone and be in the Presence of peace and joy, not for powers! Be content with whatever power, skill or talent that God gives you. Know that what He gives you and when He gives it to you will be best for your highest growth."

"Most people don't wish for powers to read minds and walk on water, but they do wish for the consolations of God, like the peace and joy and wisdom of God. When we don't get at least those consolations and small rewards for our meditations, we can feel discouraged. Do not allow yourself to be discouraged. Discouragement is one of Satan's most powerful weapons to keep us away from the peace and bliss of God. He wants to draw our attention outward. He will tell us that we are wasting our time in meditation, that it is useless to sit in the Silence. He will say that you are only human and it's too hard to meditate, that you need to rest more. He will have you believe that I am special, and I am the only son of God and that you should just take it easy! That is the lazy man's way out and it leads nowhere."

"Satan, the Dark Side, is also known to some as delusion, maya or duality. He does not often appear in a form but he is easy to recognize. Know that it is he when you feel discouraged or distracted in meditation. It is he when memories of the past arise or hopes and fears of the future when they distract us from our focus on God alone. Even beware of beautiful ideas or creative thoughts during meditation because these can be distractions for us also."

"Another way the Dark Side can get to us is with the thought that we are unworthy. You are just as worthy as any one is! We have all made mistakes. We will keep making mistakes until we are fully anchored in God, just hopefully we make fewer as we become wiser. You may be tempted to think that you are not good enough to deserve bliss yet, but this is not your first life! Remember that you have had many lives, more lives than you can count. Even the beggar in the street may be learning his last lesson! Judge no one, not even yourself!"

"One day, if you keep meditating as best as you can and calling upon God to come to you, your good karma from past lives and the good karma from this life will be enough to earn the great joy that you seek in God. This is called Samadhi. [35]
Your consistent, urgent Divine longing will be fulfilled."

"Know that there is always the Grace of God. He loves you and wants to help you return Home. Who knows when your devotion for God and your love for yourself and others will lift that thin veil that separates you from God?"

"Yes, it is alright to focus on me because I give your love for me to the Father. As your Guru, God has also given me the power to help you and multiply your spiritual efforts. I have walked the Path to God, so it is not wrong or idol worship, if you are inspired by me to be good and follow the Divine Path. But remember, we are all children of God. I am not unique from you, except that I have worked very hard, through incarnations, disciplined myself with regular meditation, prayer and serving others and sometimes fasting. I continually strive to increase my love for my Father God in all ways. You too can do the same; put God first in your lives and always strive to do His Will."

"Again, I say that you are all daughters and sons and children of God, just like me, when you do His will. You don't quite believe it yet that you are Divine and don't yet express it in your lives. Never give up your good resolutions but be patient with yourselves; you are still learning. As they say in India, *'banat, banat, ban jai'* which means 'striving, striving, one day behold: the Divine Goal!'"

"It is not enough to talk about God and read about God in the Torah. Many of the Pharisees do that much. We can't just learn from teachers and books alone; we must experience God in meditation. Then a flood of Divine Love and Wisdom will begin to flow through us."

"So, dear ones, as your chosen Guru, this is my greatest gift to you all – meditation – to introduce you directly to the Divine Father, Mother, your Eternal Friend and Beloved of your soul."

"Remember, in my oneness with our Father God, I am also your Eternal Friend and beloved of your soul – through all the ages. I give you my unconditional love and loyalty always."

So that is what I remember of his dear advice!

And now, miracle of miracles, I can meditate too! That first morning when I saw my Master Yeshua meditating, I was awe-struck with reverence and I thought that he was totally unique in all the world. Well, he really is unique in all the world but now I know, as he taught me, that I too can feel and experience the Beloved God of bliss in my own mind and soul! I simply need to consistently practice, asking for God's grace and help!

## AFTERWORD

I sincerely hope that you enjoyed reading
*Yeshua: The Stories of Jesus* and feel inspired.
My intention has been to portray Jesus or Yeshua
as the kindest, the most approachable,
the dearest of friends.

I firmly believe that in his omnipresence, he loves us all,
will never desert any one of us, that he fully understands
our failures and mistakes and brokenness.
He will always support the unique part of the One God
that each of us is and if we want help and ask for it,
he can help us regain our Divine wholeness.

I believe that he will support and multiple
our every effort to be more spiritual
and follow spiritual principles,
no matter what our religion or
beliefs or culture.

Thank you, dear reader, for reading
*Yeshua: Stories of Jesus the Christ*
and blessings on your Spiritual Path!

# BIBLIOGRAPHY

Bossis, Gabrielle. *He and I (Lui Et Moi* in the original French.) Beauchesne et ses Fils. 23) Translated to English by Evelyn M. Brown, Editions Paulines, 1969.

Douglas, Lloyd C. *The Robe.* Houghton Mifflin Co., 1942.

Foresee, Alysea. *Stories of Jesus.* Unity School of Christianity, 1955. (Out of print and in the public domain.)

Dowling, Levi. *The Aquarian Gospel. Dover Public., 1908.*

*Parellel Bible - King James Version / Modern English Version. Passio Publishinig, 2014.*

Yogananda, Paramahansa. *Autobiography of a Yogi.* Self-Realization Fellowship, 1946, 12th edition 1981.

Yogananda, Paramahansa. *Second Coming of Christ: The Resurrection of the Christ Within You.* Self-Realization Fellowship, 2004.

Yogananda, Paramahansa. *The Yoga of Jesus: Understanding the Hidden Teachings of the Gospels.* Self-Realization Fellowship, 2007.

## FROM THE INTERNET

Translation and transliteration of **the Lord's Prayer in Aramaic** are by Neil Douglas-Klotz from his book -
*Desert Wisdom: A Nomad's Guide to Life's Big Questions from the Heart of the Native Middle East*. ARC books. 2011. Reprinted with permission. For further information, go to Abwoon Network: *www.abwoon.org*

# STUDY NOTES

I totally enjoyed writing this little book. One of my favorite chapters is Chapter 14 "Yeshua's Trip to India". It took the longest to write, the most study and thought. I was finally able to finish it on the plane returning from my pilgrimage to Israel.

I have been so inspired by Paramahansa Yogananda's

### *Autobiography of a Yogi*

In this book, I received my inspiration for the Three Wise Men, as follows:
*Balthazar* from the description of *Mahavatar Babaji* in Chapter 33,
*Melchior* from the description of *Lahiri Mahasaya* in chapters 31, 32 and 34 and
*Gaspar* from the description of *Sri Yukteswar Giri* in chapter 12.

Yogananda's descriptions of saints that he met, such as those described in chapters 9, 39 and 46, to name just a few, are very inspiring. As you can probably guess, it is my favorite book.

Another great inspiration for me was Paramahansa Yogananda's book:

### *The Second Coming of Christ:*

### *The Resurrection of the Christ Within You*

I love his thoughts on the Lord's Prayer and its esoteric meaning and perspective in Discourses 28 and 54.

I learned more about "The Birth of Jesus and the Adoration of the Three Wise Men" in Discourse 3 and its footnotes.

You can buy one or both of these books or e-books at

*http://bookstore.yogananda-srf.org/*

If you are interested in Nicholas Roerich's Diary *Jesus's Eastern Travels* and his visit to the Hemis Buddhist Monastery in Ladakh, Nepal, please see Appendix 1 for a portion of it.

Paramahansa Yogananda comments about the visit to the Hemis monastery in his book *The Second Coming of Christ, Discourse 5, page 82.*

Yogananda also describes in *Discourse 5, p 81 – 89,* the challenges Yeshua faced in India, why he went to India and he comments on Nicholas Notovich's book:

*The Unknown Years of Jesus' Life – Sojourn in India*

I further cherish Gabrielle Bossis' *He and i*, a book of her conversations with the Lord Jesus that she received with her divine intuition. Although her book was first written in French and from a Catholic point of view, I deeply appreciate the devotional habit of Practicing the Presence of God as Jesus or Yeshua.

For a sample of *her He and i* quotes, see Appendix 2.

Because of her book, I had the courage to begin asking inner questions of the Divine and receiving inner answers that are the basis of these stories.


The final chapter I entitled "Memories of Meditating with the Master". Most of the ideas that I have written are from Self-Realization Fellowship Convocation summer classes in Los Angeles that I have attended over the years. I hope that you are able to attend one someday because it is absolutely amazing to meditate with 3,000 people and learn spiritual truths for a whole week from the monks and nuns!

There are many beautiful ways to meditate, if you want to learn. One lovely online option which has tips with audio and visuals supports and home study lessons is:

*https://yogananda.org/*


May your spiritual study and meditations, wherever the Path leads you, be rich and deeply satisfying and bring you peace, bliss and enlightenment.


Sincerely,


*Maudeen Grace Jordan*

# FURTHER STUDY NOTES

# IN RELATIONSHIP TO FOOTNOTES

*All of these footnotes refer to spiritual principles and not to exact quotes with the exception of numbers 9 and 22, as follows:*

*The following footnote refers to The Lord's Prayer translations from:*

> *Neil Douglas-Klotz, <u>Desert Wisdom: A Nomad's Guide to Life's Big Questions from the Heart of the Native Middle East</u>. ARC books. 2011. Reprinted with permission. For further information, go to Abwoon Network: www.abwoon.org*

*9 - The Lord's Prayer in the original Aramaic and an English translation –* www.abwoon.org

*The following footnote references a quote from:*

> *Bossis, Gabrielle. <u>He and i</u> (<u>Lui Et Moi</u> in original French.) Beauchesne et ses Fils. 23) Translated to English by Evelyn M. Brown, Editions Paulines, 1969.*

*22 - Intimate Friend –* page 62 or July 17, 1939.

*There are more exact quotes from the book <u>He and i</u> in Appendix II.*

*The following footnotes refer to spiritual principles in the book:*

> *Yogananda, Paramahansa. <u>Autobiography of a Yogi</u>. Self-Realization Fellowship, 1946, 12<sup>th</sup> edition 1981.*

*3 – Meditation* – chapter 14

*4 - Single or Spiritual Eye* – chapters 39, 45

*15 - Animals* – chapter 27

*21 - Compassion* and *Forgiveness* –
chapters 13 and 44, pages 431 – 432

*35 - Meditation, Kriya Yoga Science, Samadhi* –
chapter 26


*The following footnotes refer to spiritual principles in the book:*

> *Yogananda, Paramahansa. <u>Second Coming of Christ: The Resurrection of the Christ Within You</u>, Self-Realization Fellowship, 2004.*

*1 - Names of Jesus in various countries* –
Discourse 5 - footnotes, page 85 - 86

*2 - Children* – Discourse 47
(See also Matthew 18:1-5 and Mark 9:33 -37)

*3 - Meditation* – Discourses 7, 8, 14

**19 - *Power of prayer* -** Discourse 28

**20 - *Law of cause-and-effect or karma* –**
Discourse 73, p 1450

**21 - *Forgiveness and compassion* –**
Discourse 27, p 467 – 468; 475 – 483

**23, 24, 25, 26, 27 - *The Three Wise Men* –**
Discourse 3 and footnotes

Please also refer to previous **Study Notes.**

**"Nicholas Roerich Diary" - *Hemis Buddhist Monastery in Ladakh, Nepal* –** Discourse 5, pg. 81 - 82

Please also refer to **Appendix I** for Selections from Nicholas Roerich's diary.

**See Yogananda's comments on Nicholas Notovich's book** The Unknown Years of Jesus' Life – Sojourn in India; and Yogananda's description of the challenges Yeshua faced in India and why he went to India – Discourse 5, pg. 81 -89

**30 - *Unconditional love of the Master or Guru***
– Discourse 9, p 189 – 190

**31 - *Guru or Master introduces the disciple to God and His Omnipresent Bliss Consciousness***
– Discourse 9, p 191 -193

**32 - Meaning of the Son of God –**
Discourse 1, p 17–18;
Discourses 15; 30; 70, p 1373 – 74

**33 - Greatest Love of All –**
Discourse 74, p 1477 – 78

**34 – Comforter –**
Discourse 70, p 1378 – 79; p 1384 – 1387

**35 - Meditation, Kriya Yoga Science and Samadhi –**
Discourse 61

*The following footnote refers to a story from the book:*

> **Dowling, Levi. The Aquarian Gospel. Dover Publications, 1908**

**28 - Yeshua puts out the house fire** – pages 126 -128

*The following footnote refers to a story from the book:*

> **Douglas, Lloyd C. The Robe. Houghton Mifflin Company, 1942.**

**29 - The woman who chose the harder path** – *(Also* see the old classic movie also called "The Robe.")

# APPENDICES

## Appendix I

*Author's note: This appendix is an account of Nicholas Roerich who visited the Himis Monastery in Tibet and found these amazing notes of Issa visit there. A portion of his notes are listed here. I included his notes as a further validation that Jesus the Christ did visit Tibet.*

Jesus's Eastern Travels
(Portions of the Roerich Diary)
by Nicholas Roerich
Source: Summit University Press

*In 1925, another Russian named Nicholas Roerich arrived at Himis. Roerich was a philosopher and a distinguished scientist. He apparently saw the same documents as Notovitch and Abhedananda. And he recorded in his own travel diary the same legend of St. Issa. Speaking of Issa, Roerich quotes legends which have the estimated antiquity of many centuries.*

. . . "St. Issa passed his time in several ancient cities of India such as Benares. All loved him because Issa dwelt in peace with Vaishas and Shudras whom he instructed and helped. But the Brahmins and Kshatriyas told him that

Brahma forbade those to approach who were created out of his womb and feet. The Vaishas were allowed to listen to the Vedas only on holidays and the Shudras were forbidden not only to be present at the reading of the Vedas but could not even look at them."

"The Vaishas and Shudras were struck with astonishment and asked what they could perform. Issa bade them "Worship not the idols. Do not consider yourself first. Do not humiliate your neighbor. Help the poor. Sustain the feeble. Do evil to no one. Do not covet that which you do not possess and which is possessed by others."

"Afterward, Issa went into Nepal and into the Himalayan mountains."

"Well, perform for us a miracle," demanded the servitors of the Temple. Then Issa replied to them: "Miracles made their appearance from the very day when the world was created. He who cannot behold them is deprived of the greatest gift of life. But woe to you, enemies of men, woe unto you, if you await that He should attest his power by miracle."

"Issa taught that men should not strive to behold the Eternal Spirit with one's own eyes but to feel it with the heart, and to become a pure and worthy soul...."

"Not only shall you not make human offerings, but you must not slaughter animals, because all is given for the use of man. Do not steal the goods of others, because that would be usurpation from your near one. Do not cheat, that you may in turn not be cheated ...."

"Beware, ye, who divert men from the true path and who fill the people with superstitions and prejudices, who blind the vision of the seeing ones, and who preach subservience to material things. "...

"Issa taught: "Do not seek straight paths in darkness, possessed by fear. But gather force and support each other. He who supports his neighbor strengthens himself."

"I tried to revive the laws of Moses in the hearts of the people. And I say unto you that you do not understand their true meaning because they do not teach revenge but forgiveness. But the meaning of these laws is distorted."

"At this time, an old woman approached the crowd, but was pushed back. Then Issa said, "Reverence Woman, mother of the universe,' in her lies the truth of creation. She is the foundation of all that is good and beautiful. She is the source of life and death. Upon her depends the existence of man, because she is the sustenance of his labors. She gives birth to you in travail, she watches over your growth. Bless her. Honor her. Defend her. Love your wives and honor them, because tomorrow they shall be mothers, and later-progenitors of a whole race. Their love ennobles man, soothes the embittered heart and tames the beast. Wife and mother - they are the adornments of the universe."

"As light divides itself from darkness, so does woman possess the gift to divide in man good intent from the thought of evil. Your best thoughts must belong to woman. Gather from them your moral strength, which you must possess to sustain your near ones. Do not humiliate her, for therein you will humiliate yourselves. And all which you will do to mother, to wife, to widow or to another woman in sorrow - that shall you also do for the Spirit."

"Near Lhasa was a temple of teaching with a wealth of manuscripts. Jesus was to acquaint himself with them. Meng-ste, a great sage of all the East, was in this temple. Finally, Jesus reached a mountain pass and in the chief city of Ladak, Leh, he was joyously accepted by monks and people of the lower class .... And Jesus taught in the monasteries and in the bazaars (the marketplaces); wherever the simple people gathered--there he taught."

"Not far from this place lived a woman whose son had died and she brought him to Jesus. And in the presence of a multitude, Jesus laid his hand on the child, and the child rose healed. And many brought their children and Jesus laid his hands upon them, healing them."

"Among the Ladakis, Jesus passed many days, teaching them. And they loved him and when the time of his departure came, they sorrowed as children."

# *Appendix II*

Here are some beautiful quotes from *He and I, the diary of Gabrielle Bossis, a Franciscan Catholic and French playwright. Yeshua or Jesus is speaking to her. I have included her diary notes as a stimulus to your own practice of the Presence of the Divine. Each one gives you a page reference but also the date when she heard or intuited these beautiful words, in her conscious mind:*

"I am perfect Poise, the same yesterday, today and forever. I am the Presence, the Loving Look. The entire cosmos is cradled in Me. I am this second of time and I am Eternity. I am the lavishness of Love, the One who calls so that you may come without fear and throw yourself upon My heart. I call. You, at least you, my child, be the response."          *He and i*, page 62 or January 17, 1940

"Keep in mind this prayer, 'Lord, deliver us from anxiety about trifles!' Everything is insignificant apart from God whose life in you, you should daily seek to increase."
*He and i*, page 87 or September 21, 1940

"Advance. Advance. Let nothing hinder your trustful step forward...Can you ever imagine that I would fail to help you reach your goal? … Alone you can't do anything. But trusting in Me, leaning on Me, submerged in Me you can do everything. That's why I keep on saying, 'Lose yourself in Me and humbly ask Me to act for you, and I'll act'."
*He and i*, page 103 or January 9,1941

"Why be so anxious about the opinion of others? Isn't Mine enough? If you are with me, let them talk. Take your place on My shoulder and forget everything."

....."Seize upon every opportunity of keeping silent and give Me this silence just as though you were picking a flower for Me. Oh, this beautiful silence full of peace, humility, serenity and intimacy with God! How much you can obtain in these blessed moments! And then there is the silencing of your thoughts and memories."

"Try. If you don't succeed one way, find another. You remember the branch of the tree that you couldn't cut down in your garden until you tried cutting from another direction? It fell by itself then. But it takes patience. Never think that you have fully succeeded."

"Aim to the best of your ability. Isn't it for God? Why should you give up? My very little girl, you must begin to be happy to suffer for Me. You know that I was happy to suffer for you. Don't two friends seek to give one another things? Would you be content to just receive?"

"Be just as gracious toward the little ones as toward the great ones. Make an effort particularly when you are with people who seem vulgar to you. Go to everyone with the same gentleness. You are all brothers in Me. Wasn't I everyone's Brother? Don't let take your eyes off your model.

*He and i*, page 81 or July 25, 1940

"Take the initiative in love. Above all, don't lose your smile. Give it to Me so that I may bless it."
*He and i*, page 202-203 or March 28, 1946


"Get out of yourself. Surrender the helm of your life to me. Let your soul be lost in Mine. Why do you want to do everything? Give Me your trust and then just let yourself drift along wherever I take you."
*He and i*, page 48 or June 12, 1938


"Plunge into the infinite ocean of peace, calm as a beautiful sunrise... Put your forehead against My forehead. Enter into My thoughts."
*He and i*, page 111 or June 5, 1941


"As for you, don't bargain with Me, but go joyously to your post when I call you. Say to yourself, 'He wants me there.' And with that, you remain courageous and at peace. You remember what courage it took Me to fulfill My mission to the very end? Imitate Me. Am I not the elder Brother, who sets an example because the Father has confided His secrets to Him? Confide in Me, My child. Tell me about yourself quite simply. I understand everything so well. You know that, don't you? And yet, I love to have you explain all your emotions and fears and desires...
*He and i,* page 208-209 or May 16, 1946.

## ABOUT THE AUTHOR

Me! Wow, I can call myself an author now! Amazing! I never expected that grace!

*I was born Maudeen Grace Anderson. I was influenced by my father Gus and my Aunt Ruth saying that I'd make a good psychiatric social worker. I did become a social worker and later a Licensed Clinical Social Worker in private practice, helping to ease life traumas and griefs.*

*I am now Maudeen Grace Jordan, married to Peter and we have one daughter. My experiences and roles in life definitely influenced me and gave me compassion and empathy in the areas of marriage, parenting, caretaking, living, forgiving oneself and carving out a meditative lifestyle, while still having a busy life.*

*Another great influence in my life was my mother. She was ahead of her time and became a Unity minister in the 1970's. I embraced the Unity teaching of Christ-in-all-individuals and in-all-religions as expressions of the One God. She also demonstrated to me that going after your goals at an older age is doable and worth the trouble.*

121

As a young adult in the 1970's, I found Self - Realization Fellowship, which has the same ideals and beliefs as Unity Church but with the further teaching of how to uncover and develop one's own Christ-consciousness. SRF teaches meditation through home-study lessons and an online website about how to go within in meditation to discover our real identity as children of God or Spirit. The lessons also include tips on living a spiritual life. I have been a member now since the 1970's.

I began writing unexpectedly after reading the book He and i by Gabrielle Bossis with its emphasis on practicing the Presence of God. I began asking questions of the Divine, in this case the Lord Jesus. The inward answers to my questions came to me mostly in the morning, upon awakening. The answers I received became the stories in this book, inspired by my love for him and my desire to make Jesus the Christ more approachable for all.

In 2018, I traveled on Pilgrimage to Israel and walked the paths where Jesus lived, taught, healed and spent his final days on Earth. What an amazing and inspiring privilege to go and actually walk where he lived and taught.

*Since that Pilgrimage, I have become a Life Coach, trying to make my life as authentically-me as possible and wanting to help others live their own authentic lifestyle and manifest their treasured goals. I still apply my counseling skills and the wonderful tool of EMDR to ease life traumas, when needed, but what a joy to focus primarily on what people want to manifest in their lives!*

*You can discover more of who I am on my website* <u>*SpiritBalancedLife.com*</u>

*If you wish to contact me about your interest in Life Coaching by Skype or phone, I welcome the chance to get to know you! I offer a free half-hour introductory session and can be reached at <u>mgracejordan@gmail.com</u>*